Contents

THE STORY OF PUSS-IN-BOOTS

Poor Tom has only his ragged clothes, a few pennies and a pet cat. Luckily for him, it's no ordinary cat ... It's Puss-in-Boots, the cleverest cat in the kingdom. Puss decides to make Tom's fortune and change him from a beggar boy into a Marquis who marries a pretty Princess.

Choose a Part

This play is a story that you can read with your friends and perhaps even act out in front of an audience. You need up to four people. Before you start choose which parts you would like to play.

These two parts can be played by one person.

King
A very grand man.

Ogre
An ugly bighead.

Puss-in-Boots
A clever cat.

Tom
A kind boy.

These two parts can be played by one person.

Storyteller
Someone who helps to tell the tale.

Princess Rose
A pretty young lady.

How many people are going to take part?

If there are four people taking part, sit together so that you can all see the book.

If there are two or three people, share out the parts between you.

If you want to read the play on your own, use a different sounding voice for each part.

Reading the Play

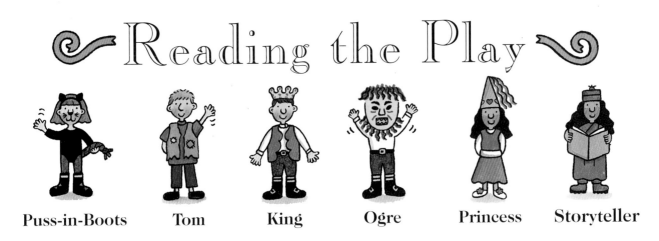

Puss-in-Boots   Tom   King   Ogre   Princess   Storyteller

The play is made up of different parts. Next to each part there is a name and a picture. This shows who should be talking.

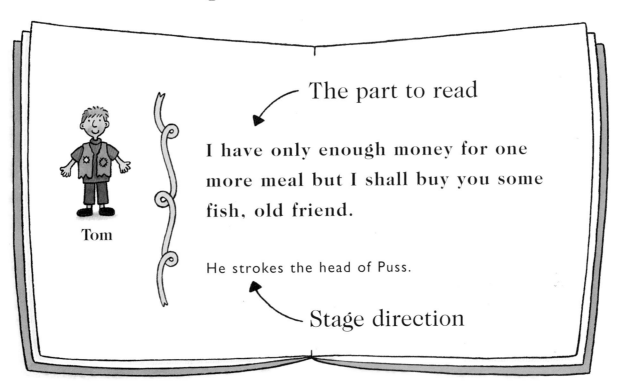

Tom

The part to read

I have only enough money for one more meal but I shall buy you some fish, old friend.

He strokes the head of Puss.

Stage direction

In between the parts there are some stage directions. They are suggestions for things you might do, such as making a noise or miming an action.

Things to Make

Here are some suggestions for dressing the part.

Tom: Clothes and Props

Tom starts off poor. Wear plimsolls and trousers and an untucked t-shirt under a ragged waistcoat. Then swop it for a grand waistcoat and tuck your trousers into shiny decorated boots.

Make a Ragged Waistcoat

You need:
- Stiff paper
- Scissors, pencil and ruler
- Tape or glue
- A t-shirt

1. Cut out three pieces of paper to make your waistcoat. Use your t-shirt as a pattern.

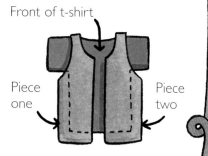

Front of t-shirt

Piece one

Piece two

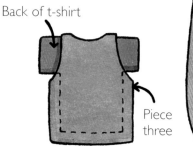

Back of t-shirt

Piece three

2. Tape or glue the pieces together as shown.

3. Cut round the edges to make the waistcoat look ragged. Draw or stick a patch on.

Make Grand Boots

You need:
- A pair of wellington boots
- Shiny sticky gift wrapping tape
- Scissors

Put a line of tape round the top of your boots and stick pieces on the front to make buckle shapes.

Make a Grand Waistcoat

Follow the ragged waistcoat instructions but cut three different-shaped pieces like this:

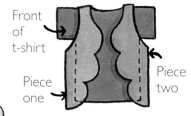

Front of t-shirt

Piece one

Piece two

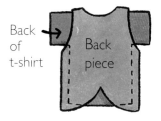

Back of t-shirt

Back piece

Decorate your grand waistcoat with shiny buttons and scrap paper.

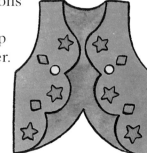

PLAYTALES

PUSS-IN-BOOTS

MOIRA BUTTERFIELD

Heinemann

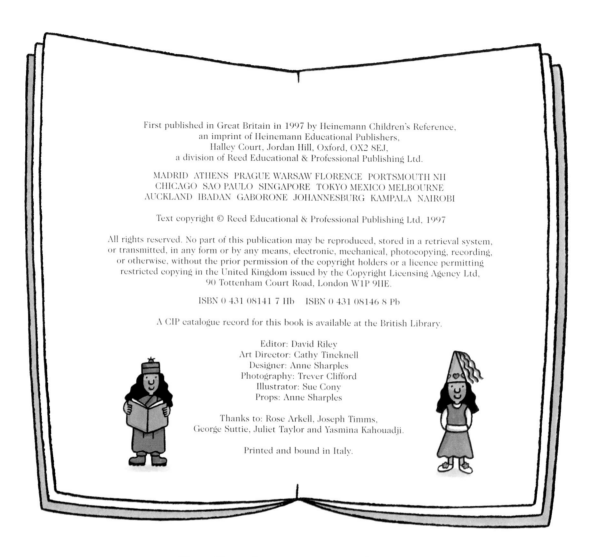

First published in Great Britain in 1997 by Heinemann Children's Reference,
an imprint of Heinemann Educational Publishers,
Halley Court, Jordan Hill, Oxford, OX2 8EJ,
a division of Reed Educational & Professional Publishing Ltd.

MADRID ATHENS PRAGUE WARSAW FLORENCE PORTSMOUTH NH
CHICAGO SAO PAULO SINGAPORE TOKYO MEXICO MELBOURNE
AUCKLAND IBADAN GABORONE JOHANNESBURG KAMPALA NAIROBI

Text copyright © Reed Educational & Professional Publishing Ltd, 1997

ISBN 0 431 08141 7 Hb   ISBN 0 431 08146 8 Pb

A CIP catalogue record for this book is available at the British Library.

Editor: David Riley
Art Director: Cathy Tincknell
Designer: Anne Sharples
Photography: Trever Clifford
Illustrator: Sue Cony
Props: Anne Sharples

Thanks to: Rose Arkell, Joseph Timms,
George Suttie, Juliet Taylor and Yasmina Kahouadji.

Printed and bound in Italy.

You will need to use scissors and glue to
make the props for your play. Always
make sure an adult is there to help you.

Use only water-based face paints and
make-up. Children with sensitive skin
should use make-up and face paints
with caution.

PUSS-IN-BOOTS: CLOTHES AND PROPS

Wear leggings or tights, and a t-shirt or leotard in grey, black or brown.
Use a large safety pin to fasten a tail to the back of your costume and
paint your face like a cat's. Wear shiny decorated wellingtons like Tom.

Make a Tail

You need:

- Three strips cut from a binliner, roughly 500mm by 80mm

1. Cut a fringe at the bottom of each strip. Knot the strips together above the fringes.

2. Wind the strips round and round each other.

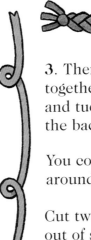

3. Then knot them together near the top and tuck the tail into the back of your belt.

You could twirl your tail around when you speak.

Cut two ears out of stiff black card and tape or glue them on to a head band.

Facepainting Ideas

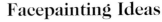

Put dots and whiskers on your cheeks. Then paint the end of your nose black and put a black line between your nose and your mouth. Make your eyes cat-shaped, if you like.

PRINCESS: CLOTHES AND PROPS

Wear a party dress and a Princess' hat.

Make a Princess' Hat

You need:

- Stiff paper or card 460mm by 620mm
- Tape and scissors
- Ribbons or crêpe paper
- Paint or coloured paper scraps to decorate the hat

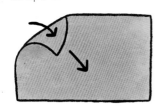

1. Roll the card down from one corner. Keep rolling to make a cone. Check it fits your head.

2. Tape the cone together and cut round the bottom to make a straight edge.

3. Tape ribbons or strips of crêpe paper to the top of the hat and decorate it any way you like.

KING AND OGRE: CLOTHES AND PROPS

Wear a shirt and trousers tucked into decorated boots. The King should wear a crown and a waistcoat like Tom's. The Ogre has a mask to wear.

Make a Crown

You need:
- Shiny card
- Scissors, pencil, glue and sticky tape
- Tape measure and ruler
- Coloured paper scraps

1. Draw a long crown pattern on the back of the card. Make it as wide as you like with points along the top edge. It should be 75mm longer than the measurement around your head.

2. Cut out the shape and decorate the front with paper scraps.

3. Tape the two ends together, overlapping them by 40mm. Check this crown fits before you put the tape on.

Make an Ogre Mask

You need:
- Scrap paper and stiff paper or thin card, 175mm by 200mm
- Scissors and pencil
- Two lengths of elastic
- Hole punch
- Paints for decoration

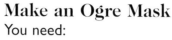

1. Make a practice mask out of scrap paper. Fold the paper in half. Draw half an oval, half a mouth and half a nose shape.

2. Cut out the mask and try it on your face for size. Mark where the eyes should be and cut them out. Then make the real one from card.

3. Decorate the mask how you like. You could stick lengths of paper round it to make hair and a beard.

4. Punch a hole on either side, just above where your ears should be. Knot the elastic through the holes so you can tie the lengths round the back of your head.

Facepainting Ideas

The King could have an elegant beard and moustache.

Stage and Sounds

Once you have read the play through you may want to perform it in front of an audience. If so, read through this section first. Rehearse the play, working out when you are going to come on and off stage, and what actions you are going to perform.

PROPS

If you like, set up four chairs to represent the inside of the King's coach. Place two chairs facing the other two chairs.

Have a bag or sack ready as a prop for Puss-in-Boots.

Position a table on-stage with a cloth over it to hide the back. Tom can pretend to swim behind this table.

ACTIONS

Puss-in-Boots should practise swirling his tail and meowing.

The Ogre should practise miming as a lion and as a mouse.

SOUNDS

Practise saying 'The Marquis of Carabas'. The first word is pronounced Mar-kwis.

If you like, get some assistants to shout off-stage as Tom appears to be drowning. Shout things like 'Catch him!' and 'Pull him out!' You could get someone to make splashing noises by slapping a wooden spoon into a bowl of water.

REHEARSING

Rehearse the play before you ask someone to watch.

The Play

Storyteller

Once upon a time there was a poor boy called Tom. All he had in the world were some ragged clothes, a few pennies and a pet cat.

The Storyteller points to Tom and Puss, who should stand together.

Puss-in-Boots

I am no ordinary cat. I can talk and I can stand up, too!

Tom

I only have enough money for one more meal but I shall buy you some fish, old friend.

He strokes the head of Puss.

Puss-in-Boots

Meow. You are a kind boy, Tom, and I'm going to make your fortune. Use your money to buy me a pair of smart boots and a sack. Don't look so surprised! Just do what I say. Always remember that cats are clever.

Tom did what Puss asked. He bought a sack and some fine boots that fitted perfectly.

COSTUME
CHANGE

Puss puts the boots on proudly.

I shall call myself Puss-in-Boots from now on.

Puss-in-Boots

The cat took Tom to the woods and filled the sack with juicy green leaves.

Storyteller

Puss-in-Boots

Sssh. Keep very quiet, Tom. Hide behind this bush and watch.

If you like, Puss and Tom can pretend to hide behind a door or table and peep out at an open bag.

Storyteller

Soon a rabbit hopped into the bag to eat the leaves. As quick as a flash, Puss pounced on the bag and closed it up.

Puss should pounce on the bag and hold it up.

Puss-in-Boots

Stay here, Tom. I'm going to take this rabbit to the palace to give to the King. The guards will let me in when they see me in my fine boots.

Puss-in-Boots turns to the King, bows and pretends to hand over a gift.

Puss-in-Boots

My master, the Marquis of Carabas, sends you this fine rabbit for your supper.

King

Thank you. How very thoughtful.

Storyteller

Then, once again, Puss went to the woods. This time he filled the sack with seeds and caught a fat partridge. He took it to the palace.

Puss bows to the King and pretends to hand over a gift.

Puss-in-Boots

I have another gift from my master, the Marquis of Carabas.

King

Your master is very kind. I'd like to meet him.

Storyteller

Puss-in-Boots told Tom what the King had said.

Tom

My clothes are in rags, Puss. I'll never be allowed through the palace doors.

Puss-in-Boots

Do what I say and you will meet the King. Today I want you to go swimming under the bridge near the palace.

Puss-in-Boots whispers into Tom's ear, as if telling him the rest of a secret plan. Tom should then take off his ragged waistcoat and hide behind a table or door, with his grand waistcoat and boots nearby.

Storyteller: Tom did what his cat asked. He hid his ragged clothes under the bridge and got into the water. Soon the King's coach came by.

Puss-in-Boots: Help! Help! The Marquis of Carabas is drowning!

King: Stop the coach! Save that man!

17

Storyteller

The King's soldiers pulled Tom out of the river. They didn't see his old rags hidden on the riverbank.

Tom

All my clothes have been stolen!

King

I'll give you new ones. It's the least I can do. I'm so glad to meet the Marquis of Carabas at last.

COSTUME CHANGE

Tom puts on his grand waistcoat and tucks his trousers into his new shiny boots.

Storyteller

Tom and Puss were given a ride in the King's coach. Inside sat the King's daughter, Princess Rose.

COSTUME CHANGE

The Storyteller puts on the Princess' hat.

Princess Rose

Tell me, do you have a castle near here?

Tom

Um, er...

Puss-in-Boots

Of course. It's just down the road. Would you like to have supper there? I shall go and prepare it.

COSTUME CHANGE — The person playing the King should take off the crown and put on the Ogre's mask, ready for their other part. The Storyteller takes off the Princess's hat.

Storyteller

> Puss-in-Boots jumped from the coach and scampered off to a nearby castle, where he knew a horrible Ogre lived.

Puss-in-Boots

> Good day, Ogre. I hear you are quite good at magic.

Ogre

> Quite good? How dare you! I'm brilliant!

Ogre

Watch me turn into a fierce lion who likes eating pussy cats!

The Ogre appears to turn into a lion and chases Puss-in-Boots round, roaring loudly.

Puss-in-Boots

I'll bet you can't change into something small, like a mouse.

The Ogre appears to become a mouse and squeaks. Puss-in-Boots chases him off-stage. Then Puss comes back on stage licking his lips.

Puss-in-Boots

I'm good at catching mice. That one was tasty.

COSTUME CHANGE

Off-stage, the person playing the King should take off the Ogre mask and put the crown back on.

Puss-in-Boots

> Ah, here comes the King's coach. Welcome to the castle of the Marquis of Carabas.

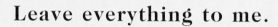

> Leave everything to me.

Puss-in-Boots
(in a loud whisper to Tom)

Storyteller

> The King and the Princess dined on the very best food and drink. Puss-in-Boots had found it all in the Ogre's kitchen.

King

You are obviously very rich, Carabas. Pass me some more caviar, would you?

Puss-in-Boots (whispers)

Tom, do you like the Princess?

Tom

I love her! Princess, will you marry me?

COSTUME CHANGE

The Storyteller puts on the Princess' hat.

Princess

Yes, dear Marquis. I loved you from the moment I saw you.

Puss-in-Boots meows and purrs.

Tom and the Princess hold hands and parade around with the King and Puss-in-Boots walking behind them in a wedding procession.

Storyteller

Soon there was a wedding and from that day on, Puss-in-Boots had the best of everything.

Tom

I still don't know how you did it, Puss.

Puss-in-Boots

Meow. Remember what I told you. All cats are clever. Meow. Pass me my bowl of cream.

Puss-in-Boots licks his lips. Then everyone bows to each other or to the audience.